A Dream Come True

Dedicated to my loving wife.

Every day you inspire me to be a better man.
This book is a small token of my appreciation.

Table of Contents

CHAPTER I

Who is that Girl?

"Love," according to most dictionaries, is defined as a "profound, tender, passionate affection for another person." Yet this definition fails to capture the reality of what actually occurs when someone finds himself or herself profoundly and confusedly lost in the act of love. Nothing will ever compare to the personal experience one feels when absolutely submerged in love.

Thus begins the tale of an eighth grader by the name of Chad, who sits idly on a random weekday in the middle of Mr. Smertzon's computer class. It was the beginning of the school year, and Chad found himself lost deep within the caverns of his own mind, aimlessly drifting from thought to thought. He lost interest in the voice of his teacher, who blurted out trivial instructions to the rest of the class, and while his mind kept on wandering, his eyes reached a certain "someone" special sitting near him in class.

A moment passed and his eyes were locked on this angelic girl. His heart made a deep thump that sprang life back into his aimless mind.

"Who is this girl?" the little voice in his head asked.

Chad was surprised when he saw that the girl was now looking right back at him! When their eyes met for the first time, it felt as if time itself stood still for Chad. He envisioned a ray of sunshine bathing this gorgeous girl; he imagined autumn leaves falling from the sky around her to frame this perfect representation of beauty. In this magical moment, the girl sent a slight smile in the direction of Chad. Just like that, the moment was gone and eye contact was lost, but as class continued, he kept on repeating to himself, "Who is that girl?"

"That girl" was none other than Alice, who had absolutely no idea of what had just occurred in Chad's pubescent loins. Her big blue eyes and her sweet vanilla scent would become the very elements that propelled young Chad into the treacherous path of love. He had opened a door from which there was no return, even though he was completely unaware of that fact.

"Chad!" a bouldering voice called out.

Within a fraction of a second, Chad was instantly back in the classroom. Mr. Smertzon asked him if he would be so kind as to assist his peers in logging onto their computers. Obviously this was a ridiculous gesture, but what can you expect from a teacher who assumes all people other than him are computer illiterate? Also, Chad realized that this would be an ideal opportunity to introduce himself to that certain "someone."

He struck up a conversation with Alice and began talking his little eighth grader heart out. It seemed that both of them really hit it off, at least in Chad's mind anyways; however, he was so nervous he couldn't even remember what they talked about. As the bell rang signaling the change between classes, he gathered his things and made his way towards Humanities class.

Another bell rang, signaling that class had now officially started and he made his way to his desk. The first thing he noticed was Alice sitting across the room, and for some reason he completely forgot about how easy it was for him to talk to her only a few minutes earlier. He started feeling queasy and had butterflies clawing at his stomach. He could hardly even make eye contact with her.

"What the hell is wrong with me?" Chad screamed inside. "Go over and say something to her!"

Before he could muster up the courage to say something, Alice walked by.

"You're kind of shy, aren't you?" she asked.

"Think of something clever and cool to say," Chad thought to himself.

"New school, new people," he said, sounding like a complete jackass!

Alice smiled and replied, "Well, now you've got a new friend."

This statement made Chad very happy indeed, and as the school day continued at a turtle's pace, a warm feeling of joy came over him. While walking home after school, he couldn't shake the feeling that was buzzing inside him. He kept remembering the way she laughed, the twinkle in her eye, and that sweet, perfect, lingering scent she left behind wherever she went; unbeknownst to Chad, his heart had, for the first time ever, been freshly pierced by Cupid's arrow.

That night he couldn't sleep as he kept thinking about that girl. He dreamt of a blossoming relationship between him and Alice. He kept seeing her smile and hearing her soft beautiful voice. He was convinced that only she could give him what he really wanted. From the first moment he saw her, he knew that he wanted to be more than friends.

As excited as he was about the thought of being with Alice, he experienced another sensation that was quite the opposite. During his galore of love stricken fantasies came what the average college student would refer to as a "buzz kill"—the thought of Alice not feeling the same way about him. He couldn't bear the idea of being rejected by her and this fear made him feel very insecure. All of a sudden Chad felt what experts, or the Red Hot Chili Peppers call, the "roller coaster of love." He never knew that you could feel both "over-joyed-shouting-on-rooftops-HAPPY," and "oh-my-God-I-think-I'm going-to-soil-myself-SCARED," simultaneously. That night he battled with his thoughts while the image of Alice never left his dreams.

The next morning he woke up to the sound of his annoying alarm clock, yet despite the fact that he didn't sleep much the night before, he was more awake than the Energizer Bunny on Red Bull. He knew that it was way too soon to ask Alice out and that he'd have to get to know her a bit more. Not to mention the fact that Chad had never asked out a girl before, and let's face it, he wasn't nearly as attractive as Alice. Chad was still waiting for puberty to run its course. Regardless, he was determined to start building that relationship. He walked to his bathroom and stared himself straight in the eyes.

With all the balls an eighth grader could muster, in front of his own mirror anyways, he said out loud, "Today you will talk to her without sounding like an idiot!"

Fired up and on a mission, he went to school a bit earlier than usual to see if he could spot when she arrived. As he walked onto the school grounds, he saw a couple of friends waiting for him. They all exchanged the official eighth grader greeting ritual and continued the male gossip circle, which in most cases ends up in roughhousing and name calling.

Just like that, Alice came and caught Chad's attention; however, once more the bipolar nature of love created an inner battle within him and this time— insecurity came out the victor.

"Tomorrow," he said to himself.

Tomorrow, as it turned out, was in fact one month, three hours, and three minutes later when Chad finally had the courage to ask Alice out. During that time Chad became friends with Alice; they would even occasionally hang out in the same circle of friends. When October came, he got up with courage and went to school early where he met with his friends. After the evolved and updated version of the eighth-grader greeting ritual, the male gossip circle commenced once more.

This time, Martin had something on his mind and he wanted the entire group to hear what he had to say.

"Guys, guess what?" Martin asked.

"I don't know … what?" Chad replied.

"No, come on, man, guess!" Martin continued.

Chad never really liked Martin to begin with; he always thought of him as quite irritating.

"No really, I don't know … what?" Chad asked.

Then Martin smiled as he dropped the bomb on the little boy's heart.

"I asked Alice out," Martin said.

In that moment, Chad's heart fell to a place where most experts on love prefer to avoid talking about. All his hopes, dreams, and love-filled fantasies violently burst into flames; yet at the same time he couldn't take his wrath out on Martin … obviously Martin didn't know how Chad felt about Alice. In fact, nobody did.

"What did she say?" Chad inquired.

"She said 'yes,' man!" Martin shouted.

"Balls," Chad thought. "I missed my shot!" Now he had to watch the love of his life dating the spawn of Satan; furthermore, he would have to endure seeing their relationship unfold if she liked Martin. As he pretended to congratulate his competitor, he could only think about Alice. He started doubting for the first time that he could actually be in love with her. Was this just one of those silly high school crushes that you hear about all the time? Yet despite all his reasoning there was one undisputed fact: he felt like someone had simply come up and kicked him in the junk.

As the year went on, Chad became very good friends with Alice. Alice enjoyed Chad's humor, and well, Chad enjoyed everything about Alice. He analyzed the relationship between her and Martin to find out what she likes and dislikes. He quickly noticed that she wasn't all too pleased with Martin most of the time, yet for some reason that Chad could not understand, they kept dating.

Chad kept on thinking, "It should be me," but he never said it out loud.

Nonetheless, he now had the opportunity to really get to know Alice, and though he was still very innocent in anything to do with love, he knew that this wouldn't be the end of all hope. He knew that if he was patient enough, he would get another chance to ask her out.

In love there are no handbooks or guides; Chad was learning by being thrown into the deepest end of the pool and hoping that he didn't sink to the bottom. Luckily for Chad, he took swimming lessons when he was a child; however, he did fail a few of them.

CHAPTER II

Change

They say that time heals all wounds, but we all know that some wounds will never heal. When it comes to wounds caused by love, the damage in some cases can be irreparable. It doesn't matter if you are the strongest or bravest man on the planet, or hell, even in the whole universe for that matter; ultimately the person who holds your heart is the one who can destroy you.

Luckily for Chad this was not the case, not yet anyway, and there was still plenty of spunk left in his love-filled fascination of Alice. Several months have passed since that chimpanzee of a person, Martin, asked out the love of Chad's heart. Since then a lot has changed for the love-struck ninth grader, including his local baseball team winning the Provincials. Chad's exceptional athletic abilities had a lot to do with this victory, which is why he was named tournament MVP; now with school celebrity status, he could expand his social circles to include … almost everybody.

All the extra attention forced him to climb out of his shell and engage with the rest of the student body. Suddenly he found himself doing things after school and finally shedding the fear of speaking in public. People respected him not only for his recent athletic achievements, but also because as it turned out, Chad was actually a decent human being. He also became very popular with the ladies, although this new development was the last thing on his mind with his sights still firmly fixed upon Alice.

You see, when a boy gets hit by the poisoned tip of Cupid's arrow, there is a long-lasting effect on the heart. No matter what you do or how hard you try, you will never be able to forget your first true love; in the case of Chad, Cupid's arrow hit a main artery and infected his whole body with an undying love for Alice. Even though there were other girls interested in expanding their gene pool with him, he was completely blind to their desires.

The friendship between Chad and Alice blossomed further as time went on. Due to his new popularity, he found himself hanging out in the same circles as her. He would always treat her respectfully, but was flirtatious as well, just to test her. Flirting became one of Chad's new and favorite pastimes. He wasn't the type of person who would devise a plan to break two people up; however, the idea of having Alice all to himself certainly made him consider it. Plus, he despised Martin, so he wouldn't really feel bad about it. However, by simply staying both near her and at the same time not too close, Chad built up his relationship with her. He was sure that after starting their friendship, they would become something more … eventually.

Every time Chad would drop Alice a compliment or say something nice to her, she refused to pay too much attention to him. Her apparently oblivious nature drove him completely mad inside; if only he knew that Alice thought that this was his normal behavior with all girls! She didn't want to read too much into his actions, even though deep inside she was a little interested. On the other hand, what Alice didn't know was that the only girl that had ever mattered to him was her, and that every day since the day that he first laid eyes on her, he only wanted to be with her. But alas, this is the nature of love, which remains a continual guessing game until the day you start pushing up daisies.

One day, sitting in Ms. Cranway's French class, Chad found himself in his usual ritual of daydreaming. This specific day he found himself in some distant dimension doing things that are too complex to explain with simple English, when he noticed Alice sitting across the room with a disgruntled look on her face. He decided to inquire as to what was going on with her by sending her a note.

"Hey, Alice, how are you? You seem down, what's up?" Chad wrote.

The note traveled to the other side of the class with the help of a few classmates, and due to Ms. Cranway's acute absentmindedness the message made its way to Alice without any problems. Chad patiently waited for her to respond, and roughly seven minutes and twenty five seconds later, the note came back to him. As he opened it and read her beautiful handwriting, his jaw almost hit his desk as it dropped to the floor.

"I can't take it anymore; it's just too difficult. I have decided to break up with Martin, and I'm really sad," Alice had written.

That moment in Chad's life was bittersweet in all its meaning. He was jumping for joy on the inside, obviously still maintaining his posture, due to the fact that the love of his life finally decided to break up with that troll, Martin. Yet just as his joy was on an all-time high, he also realized that Alice was upset. Since he couldn't go to her immediately and give her a comforting hug, which he longed to do, he mustered up every bit of compassion he had for her and sent it her way through a long and sweet look. She noticed that Chad was really there for her and she counted herself lucky to be his friend.

Another lesson Chad learned that fateful day is that when one is in love, the joys and sorrows of your loved one become your own. Even though Alice wasn't aware of the fact that Chad was suffering with her in secret, she did realize that there was much more to him than what she first thought. Maybe he was more than just a good buddy.

Chad vowed that he would not waste a second this time; he understood that this was the moment he had been waiting for and that it would require action. He wanted to make her feel good again. That is all he ever wanted, regardless of if they were ever going to be together. Frequently Alice would receive a caring note from Chad, which certainly helped her get over Martin. Chad also understood that he had to time things just right, so that he didn't end up becoming the rebound guy. At the same time, he couldn't wait long enough for another troll to come in and steal his precious Alice away again.

It wasn't long before other people in the school started noticing the amount of effort Chad was investing in Alice, and soon the walls began to whisper. For some kids, it was completely insane to be so lovesick about someone else at this point in their lives, and others were amazed about how one boy could care so much about one girl. The only thing that was on Chad's mind was, "This girl; she's definitely the one!"

It's a very rare occurrence when a boy at such a young age manages to find that one true love, the one that lasts forever. However, whether Chad liked it or not, his heart belonged to Alice, whether she knew it or not.

It wasn't too long after the flood of sweetness from Chad that Alice realized there might be something more to this young man than what she originally thought. All of a sudden she started having feelings for him; not strong feelings, but strong enough to make her interested. At the same time, she felt confused because as it turned out, Chad had become her best male friend, the one she shared most of her secrets with. Gradually she began to consider him as more than a friend, which was not exactly that same arrow of love which had struck Chad. Often when people spend so much time together, like and love can get confused, and although Chad would have wanted her to feel the same way as he did about her, it wasn't the case … for now.

Later that year, after some serious contemplation, and chickening out a few times, Chad walked up to Alice in an awkward and uncomfortable way. She noticed right away that there was something very different about him. Was he was sort of nervous, or shyly confident? To Alice, he looked goofy and cute at the same time. Even though Chad was beginning to sweat and felt like he was going to throw up, he was ready for his big moment:

"Alice, would you like to go out with me one of these days? Maybe to a movie or to grab a bite to eat?" he asked.

She remained quiet for a few minutes and mulled over his request. Obviously at this moment in time, Chad was about to jump right out of his skin in suspense, and the little voice inside of him was having a full-blown panic attack! He wondered if he had come on too strong … ? Quickly, he tried to recover any chance he may have lost before it was too late.

"I know this might sound kind of random, and I don't want you to feel pressured or anything like that, but I think it would be cool to go out and get to know each other better. Want to do something this Friday?" he asked.

He didn't want to sound too pushy, but he also knew that remaining quiet was the last thing he wanted. He teetered on this precarious moment of do or die, and the silence of Alice was making him go crazy.

Just before he could say another word she responded, "Yes, this Friday sounds perfect."

In that magical moment, Chad was the happiest boy on the planet; he was over the moon. After all this time of watching Martin screw up his relationship with Alice, it was finally his turn to show her what it meant to truly love someone.

"Can we go to the Bread Garden at Rutherford Mall?" she added.

Chad simply nodded in return, as he was afraid of sounding way too excited to answer her. She then nodded back, turned and walked away. What neither of the two actually understood was that both of them felt equally excited and scared about the date to come. It was almost as if all the stars had aligned for that specific moment, when they blissfully exchanged puppy love filled smiles and went their separate ways.

On the way home, Chad was running around in his head like a toddler who had way too much candy. There was a new energy beaming through his face, and he felt truly happy after finally proving himself as a man, in his mind anyways. This happiness was very different and very new to him; he knew that this was the start of something that would change his life forever … he just didn't know how much.

CHAPTER III

The First Date

When we fall in love with someone, there is always a very awkward phase in the beginning of the relationship. Neither party knows what to expect or what each other's boundaries are yet, so they tip toe around each other, hoping not to scare away the person they love the most in the world. (This is how Chad felt anyways.)

Chad was more excited about his very first date with Alice than he had ever been about anything before, yet he was also more nervous than a piece of buttery toast at Fat Camp. School was unusually long for him that day because of a clock slowly counting down inside his head to "date time." He spoke a bit with Alice at school, but it wasn't about anything exceptional; he was awkwardly nervous and probably seemed a bit drunk.

His biggest problem came when he got to his house and was suddenly completely flabbergasted about what he was to wear, whether he should bring a gift, or even what he'll be talking about on his date! Over thinking situations is a problem Chad has had all of his life. He had never felt so jittery, not even before a big game; meanwhile the clock kept on moving forward as he prepared himself for what he felt was the biggest night of his life. Right before Chad left his house, he looked in the mirror, told himself, "You da' man," and went out the door on his way to the bus stop.

He arrived only a few minutes earlier than Alice, which made him look like a dependable guy, at least in his mind. That night she looked even more beautiful than she ever had before. He was astonished and almost left speechless as he couldn't stop staring. Alice was wearing jeans and a dark blue top with one sleeve. It was nothing overly fancy, but just the simple fact that she was there to go on a date with Chad made her look astonishing. As she came close to him, his knees started to quiver. One quick smell of that vanilla perfume was almost enough to make Chad pass out in excitement.

"Shall we?" he mumbled.

"We shall," she responded with a slight smile.

Just like that, they officially embarked on their first date. When they arrived at the restaurant, he decided to sit right next to her at the table as opposed to sitting opposite from her. It didn't matter that the waiter looked at him funny; he didn't care about what anyone else in the room might have thought. All Chad cared about was being as close to Alice as possible without seeming like a freak. He pretended not to be too eager, or so he thought, but he always attempted to get a bit closer with a slight shift here and a small nudge there.

He was so in love with her that he couldn't take his eyes off of her. He was lost in her perfect vanilla scent which lingered all around him; the only problem was that Alice didn't realize how much Chad actually liked her—but that is how love goes.

"May I take your orders?" the waiter kindly asked.

Ignoring everyone around them, both of them stared at the menu for a while. While Alice was figuring out what she wanted to order, Chad's gaze drifted to her and he forgot the menu in his hands. Suddenly, she made up her mind.

"Umm … I'd like the chicken caesar salad and an iced tea please," she replied.

Her response snapped Chad out of his hypnotic state and he realized that it was his turn to order. He had not actually studied the menu at all, since he preferred to study Alice. In order to pretend as if he had already made a thoughtful selection, he quickly scanned the menu and simply blurted out the first item that caught his eye.

"I'll take the lasagna and an iced tea as well," he answered.

The waiter looked slightly amused as he wrote down their order and left the table. Now they were alone again, and it was time to get into a decent conversation. Being only 14, this was a lot harder than you would assume. They were both feeling awkward as they realized that their close friendship was on the brink of becoming something more, and neither one of them wanted to mess it up. Both of them were almost painfully careful about what they said, and if they only would have realized that they could simply continue building on their existing relationship, the tension might have dropped. However, new love is often tormented by doubt and confusion, and so they both continued nervously with their conversation.

Just as Chad was about to run out of intelligent things to say, he was finally saved by the waiter's delivery of their meal. The beauty of being on a dinner date is that there are certain moments when silence is a must, such as when you have your mouth jam-packed with lasagna! The food helped ease the tension and eventually the date became more casual as both of them relaxed.

After dinner, they continued on with their plan and headed to the movies on the other side of the mall. The best choices appeared to be all sold out, and Alice suggested that they watch Instinct starring Anthony Hopkins and Cuba Gooding Jr. Upon entering the theatre, they began to be pessimistic due to the fact that it looked as barren as the Sahara desert. Yet nonetheless, they sat down and decided to watch anyways. Chad couldn't have cared less what they watched. It wasn't like he was going to pay attention to the movie. True to their first guess, the movie was terrible; yet any scary movie has its advantages on a first date. In Chad's mind, the movie wasn't scary enough to be able to really get close to her, in fact, it was more creepy and twisted, but in the end it was reason enough for him to reach out and touch her sweet, angelic hand.

The moment that he touched her hand, he felt this energy of excitement flow through his body. He worried that his hand might feel clammy to her, and then he worried further about becoming too aroused. Once again, Chad was over thinking the situation. Luckily, he kept his calm and made it through the end of the movie, hand in hand.

As the closing credits started rolling, Chad and Alice made their way back through the mall to their separate buses. The whole walk back they kept on throwing romantic stares and innocent smiles at each other. The anticipation of the inevitable goodbye was building, and finally they reached their departure point. Chad and Alice stood almost completely alone underneath the blanket of stars and spontaneously they shared a hug. The moment their bodies touched there was instant chemistry, and Chad could not help but seize the opportunity by throwing in a sweet kiss on Alice's lips. To his surprise and delight, she failed to resist once more and he knew that this first date was a complete success. Their first kiss, which only lasted for a couple of seconds, was the perfect culmination of their very first official date. Chad was instantly thrown on cloud nine as he saw his sweet Alice ride off in the distance.

As he waited for his bus to arrive, he could only think about Alice: how wonderful she looked, how soft her lips were, and how much he was stark-raving mad about her. He knew that tonight it would be near impossible to fall asleep, but at the same time he couldn't wait to dream about her.

It's amazing how a simple kiss can transform a young man into a wild lunatic, but this is the fate of all those brave enough to fall in love. They say that a man in love can achieve anything, and in the case of Chad, they might have a point.

CHAPTER IV

Overreacting

Sometimes when a boy is infatuated by a girl, his heart can overpower his mind. This is more commonly dubbed as "blinded by love." His mind focuses only on satisfying his heart's desires and becomes a slave to love, but this enchantment doesn't last forever and eventually reason is restored once more. There is also another body part of a young man that can overpower his mind and cause him to do all sorts of strange things, but that is the case for all men of all ages, and it requires no further discussion.

Chad was experiencing being blinded by love as his newly formed relationship with Alice was blossoming, as much as ninth grade relationships go anyway. They would hold hands and exchange innocent kisses whenever they had the chance. They knew summer was coming, and they were both going to be very busy. Chad played baseball almost the entire summer, and Alice visited family, went sailing and had a summer job.

Alice's mom worked for an eye doctor, and she managed to find Alice a job where she could file papers and do trivial office work. Alice didn't mind too much, since it gave her something to keep her busy during the long summer break and some extra money to do whatever she pleased with.

Chad was busy with his baseball team as they were making quite a racket all over the province. He had to be away on weekends, which created conflict between him and Alice's schedules. To compensate they tried to call each other as much as they could.

They spent little time together at the beginning of the summer due to their busy schedules. Every now and then Chad accompanied Alice to her Dad's house where they could spend a bit of time together, but due to the strict nature and lame rules of her father, these moments were also quick to pass. They continued dating and had a couple of memorable dates. Chad was still very green in the ways of love, and confusion sat on his heart like an uninvited guest, refusing to leave. He was absolutely and utterly in love with Alice, yet at the same time he was always afraid of doing something wrong to ruin his new relationship. Any boy his age, swimming neck deep in something he knows nothing about, normally feels this way, but the fact that Alice always seemed a lot cooler about the entire ordeal made him even more nervous.

As the summer break came into full swing, Chad and Alice saw each other less. When she left on her sailing trip with her Mom and Step-dad, she was out of town for two weeks. During that time, Chad was surprised that he hadn't heard from her at all. He could have considered that she was on a sailboat and perhaps had trouble getting to a phone. Or he could have thought that she was busy enjoying her vacation. Instead his mind went in a completely different direction. He felt rejected. In his mind, if he was away for two weeks, he would try to call as much as he could as he would miss Alice dearly. Even though Alice technically did not do anything wrong, Chad's mind went from floating on cloud nine to sinking deep into the insecure pit of rejection. His mind fabricated a fictitious scenario that screamed, "She doesn't feel the same way about you, Chad!"

As this thought began to take hold, he could hear the crackling sound of his heart breaking. In this ignorant pain, he made a decision that some would consider completely insane and irrational, but at the time he felt it had to be done. He decided that since she didn't feel the same way about him as he did about her, he would break up with her when she got back. Somehow in the mind of this little, soon-to-be-tenth-grade boy, he believed that he had to end the relationship before she did so that they could somehow remain good friends. He knew he had to start over and work harder to win her heart for good. If there was a rule book for love, Chad would have broken every rule that existed in that book.

The day that Alice returned from her trip, Chad decided to call her. He was nauseously nervous because he knew that he was going to break up with her, and he had no control over how she would react. The phone rang once and Chad could hear his heart beating in his ears, and as it rang a second time, he felt just how dry his mouth was, and just before the phone was about to give its third ring, he heard her voice.

"Hello?" Alice answered.

"Hey, Alice, it's Chad! How are you?" he asked nervously.

"Just got back, actually," she responded.

"Really, how was the trip?" he asked nervously.

"It was surprisingly good. We all had a great time. What have you been doing?" she inquired.

He paused for a second, preparing to break the news. His heart was really pounding hard this time around and each second felt like an eternity as he mustered up his courage.

"I have to tell you something," he said in a lower tone, almost as if he was swallowing his words.

Alice, quite puzzled with how Chad was speaking, simply asked, "What is it?"

He knew that now was the time to spill it; there was no turning back. The little cowardly voice inside him said, "Save yourself; protect your heart! You can't handle the pain anymore," and just like that he came out and said it.

"I think … I think it's better that we become just friends again," Chad blurted out.

After a pause he added, " … I think we were much better off when we were friends; we had a lot of fun together and it was never awkward. I just think we shouldn't rush into anything too quickly … you know?"

On the other end of the phone, Alice had a puzzled look. "What did I do?" she thought.

Chad didn't know that the mind of a woman is stranger than any fiction novel ever written throughout all time. It makes less sense than quantum physics and is more complex than a thousand NASA space stations. What he didn't realize was that he was sending messages of self-doubt and rejection to Alice. Alice felt completely blind-sided. She thought that Chad really liked her, and in her mind they were still doing okay, going out and having fun. His words truly surprised her, but she decided to respect his decision. She enjoyed spending time with Chad, but she did not feel anywhere near the way that he did. Being friends is all she ever wanted to begin with.

"Chad, you know we'll always be friends, and I care about you. So… ok, let's go back to being friends; maybe it's better that way," she said quietly.

After a long discussion, they both agreed that it was better for them to be friends again. They fed each other's disappointment with ill-fated logic that seemed to make sense for them in their own world. Their relationship reverted back to the status of friends and they only hung out a couple of times for the remainder of the summer.

It seemed that Alice adjusted quickly to the change in their relationship, but for Chad it was quite the opposite. This time it felt worse for him than it had when Martin went out with Alice, because he was the man who had messed up this time, yet despite his self-pity and shattered heart, he was determined to win her back again eventually, and this time for good. They saw each other occasionally but there was more distance between them now, which is only natural after a break up. At least this relationship ended amicably, so picking up where they left off on their friendship was not too difficult to achieve.

After summer, they went back to school and continued with their activities. They would say "hi" to each other and talk whenever they could, but their social lives were not that connected anymore. Alice focused a lot on school and kept her mind on her studies, whereas Chad decided to embrace a more social experience with a complete disregard for schoolwork. November came along and he got to meet his brand new baby brother; thankfully, the arrival of his new sibling actually helped him forget his pain and kept his mind occupied on other things.

Love's roller coaster can lead you from the most beautiful mountain top to the dirtiest gutter you have ever seen in a very short period of time. His determination to win over his Alice's heart one day, fueled by love, was leading to a long chain of unexpected events that neither of them could have predicted.

CHAPTER V

Jealousy and Love Go Hand-in-Hand

When you are deeply in love, it is an experience that can enhance the best, or the absolute worst, in you. Love often also brings out jealousy in a person. This is something that Chad had never experienced before … until now.

With the tenth grade in full swing, it seemed that the events of the previous summer were already a distant memory. Chad managed to continue to climb the social ladder and finally became one of the most popular kids in school. He was known by everyone, especially the ladies.

His relationship with Alice had regressed back to a good friendship, which was important since they shared a lot of the same friends. One day Chad went over to Alice and commented on how nice it was that even though they had dated for a few months, they could still become friends once more. He reminded her that he actually cared deeply for her and would always be there if she needed anything. Secretly, he always thought they would be the perfect couple, but he couldn't simply tell that to her. Chad also told her that if she decided to go out with another guy, he would help her find someone who would treat her like the goddess she was (this was a case of Chad simply speaking before thinking—as if he was going to help her find a different boyfriend!). He stated that he only had one condition: under no circumstance should she ever go out with Martin, who was still a troll, ever again. As the conversation came to its end, he felt that he had set the record straight and didn't have to worry that Martin would step into the picture again. What Chad didn't realize was that Alice did not like the fact that he made a condition at all. She felt that she would do damned well whatever she pleased.

Roughly two weeks later, there was a massive dance at the Millennium building in Boban Park. The dance basically consisted of a meshing up of several other high schools, which made the attendance huge. One can only imagine what happens when you mix a bunch of horny teenagers, a lot of alcohol, and a Friday night.

As usual, Chad was having the time of his life at the dance; he was experimenting with other girls by dancing, kissing, and flirting up a storm as his tenth-grader hormones led the way. He enjoyed himself to an extent, but none of the girls made him feel the way that Alice did. While he was distracted with the wide array of tail that was to be found everywhere, he failed to notice Alice anywhere around.

Finally, Alice spotted Chad from across the building as he danced the night away with a big smile planted on his face. She thought the reason he was smiling was because he had moved on and outgrown his puppy love towards her; little did she know that the only reason he was smiling was because he could hardly focus on his surroundings in his blissfully intoxicated state. Either way, the thought of him having moved on made her feel lonely and sad; she actually thought that he really liked her. She was never truly in love with Chad, but she liked the fact that he was in a state of euphoria whenever she was near. As her slight sadness over the thought of losing her not-so-secret admirer was at its peak, a certain someone also entered the building to seize the opening: Martin.

She spotted Martin as he came in and with the turn of a head they both made eye contact. He gave her a flirtatious smile which made her completely forget about her loss of Chad's interest. Knowing that Alice was single, Martin asked her to dance and shortly afterwards they were having a great time together. Meanwhile, Chad was oblivious to what was happening due to two reasons: he had way too much alcohol in his system, and too many skirts were located in his immediate area. Eventually he was struck by an uneasy feeling inside him which he knew wasn't the booze anymore, and he began scouting the room. He then saw something that made him feel like he was just kicked in the gut by a donkey.

He spotted Alice and Martin burning it up together on the dance floor. For the rest of the evening, he kept his eyes on them and saw how they were rekindling their old relationship right in front of his eyes. Chad saw Martin and Alice not only dance together, but also kiss and hold hands as if they were already boyfriend and girlfriend again. To top it off, the DJ announced on the microphone that things were about to get more "intimate," and suddenly the song "Killing Me Softly" started to play. The irony of the song was too much for Chad to handle, so he decided to leave before they did. He felt as if a piece of his heart had gone up in flames.

When Chad made his way to school the following Monday, he was not prepared to hear what his friend Jonathon came running up to tell him.

"Hey, Chad! Chad!" Jonathon screamed from a few yards away. "You know what I heard from Skyler and Ashlyn?

"What?" he responded.

"You're not going to like it," Jonathon replied.

"Well, out with it then!" he said.

"Alice and Martin are getting back together," Jonathon said.

Jonathon knew that Chad loved Alice, but he thought that it would be best for him to hear the news sooner rather than later. Chad, on the other hand, didn't say anything else to Jonathon; he remained quiet as he kept on walking. What Jonathon couldn't see was how extremely enraged Chad was at that moment. It wasn't just the fact that Alice was seeing someone else that pissed him off, but rather that she was seeing none other than the royal pain in the ass who she had promised that she would never see again. Betrayal was the first emotion to penetrate Chad's heart, which was followed by its evil twin brother, jealousy. Chad decided to write Alice a note in class, just to let her know how he felt about it.

Dear Alice,

I thought that you didn't like Martin; if I recall correctly you called him a 'moron' or an 'idiot.' The only reason I broke up with you was because I didn't think you felt the same way about me as I did about you. Why the hell would you go back to that jerk? Didn't you hate him; isn't he the biggest loser on earth?

Chad

As the note made its way to Alice, he hoped that the message would knock some sense back into the woman he loved to realize that Martin was not the right guy for her. When the note reached Alice, she opened it and Chad looked to see her reaction; to his surprise, she remained calm and collected and started writing a response. She sent the note back without even turning to look at Chad, which made him feel very insecure and nervous. Once he opened the note it read:

> Chad,
>
> I'm sorry, but I don't feel the same way about you as you feel about me, and there is nothing I can do to help that. We're not dating anymore, so I can date whomever I want. Stay out of my business!
>
> Alice

This message hit him like a ton of bricks and his heart sank to the floor. His anger started to rise soon afterwards. "How could she?" he screamed inside. His intentions might have been pure but, sadly, in his inexperienced tenth grade mind he didn't have the tact to deal with the situation adequately. He only wanted to protect her from being hurt by that douchebag Martin again. Furious, he took the note, crushed it in his hand and threw it away.

As the tenth grade continued on, Chad and Alice never uttered a word to one another, even though their lockers were only two spaces away from each other. Jealousy had twisted their love and friendship into passionate rage, and to make matters worse, they both still shared the same social spheres and had to see each other every single day, except weekends. Any passing observer would conclude that the tension could be cut with a knife. They never spoke ill of each other; in fact, they just never spoke to one another. The easiest way to deal with this situation was simple ignorance.

Chad was devastated and seeing Alice only reminded him of his pain. The most horrible moment of his day was seeing the woman he loved stand only a few feet away without being able to utter a "hello" to her. He missed their talks, her sense of humor, her perfectly shaped body, and her rosy lips. He still got to smell her perfume every day, but now it was like that sweet vanilla scent was only stabbing his heart. Every time he would see her at a party or in school, his longing only intensified, leaving him bitter on the inside. Although most people thought that they had grown apart, he was only drawn more to her.

To avoid looking weak, he continued to put up a tough front and flirt with other girls when Alice was around. His pain was so deep that he jumped from female to female and soon started to build a reputation of being a ladies' man. Girls were disposable to Chad, and every weekend he would have a new one with him. Most of these girls were completely fine with that, as this was the type of relationship they enjoyed. Some of his friends started calling him things like "Gigolo," "Don Juan," and on one occasion "Slutty Mc-Sluts." Regardless of his playboy reputation and excessive partying, there was still something very wrong inside.

Even though he enjoyed being with different girls, he would give it all up in a heartbeat if he could fix things with Alice again. He missed their friendship and the way that she laughed at his stupid jokes.

One day after thinking long and hard about their current, non-existent relationship he decided: "If I can't date her, I would at least like to become friends again." Chad just wanted her in his life any which way because her presence simply made him happier. He realized how empty his life had become, how his relationships with girls were meaningless, and that the only real thing he had going for him was Alice. He decided to swallow his pride and write a note to apologize for his idiotic behavior.

Dear Alice,

I know I have been acting like a jerk lately, and I hate what we have become. I hope you can forgive me and that we can work past all of this. I truly love you very much and all I want to do is protect you. I know I showed it in an immature way, but I want to begin to show you that I do respect and care for you.

So please forgive me for being an ass, and I also apologize for the fact that our relationship didn't work out the way we wanted it to. I hope you can forgive me and I hope even more that we can go back to being friends.

Chad

After drenching the note with every drop of emotional integrity he had, he sent it off to Alice. He didn't know what to expect in return, as they haven't been talking for quite some time now. He eagerly waited for the reply.

Dear Chad,

I'm not going to lie and say that I wasn't hurt, but we are both to blame for our relationship not working. I think it was very mature of you to send me this note and I always wanted to be your friend. I just hope you can respect the fact that I am with Martin; I'm seeing a different side of him now.

We can always be friends and I would like nothing better.

Your friend,
Alice

After reading it over and over again, dissecting every little word in the note, Chad finally made peace with the fact that the love of his life was going out with Martin. He wasn't sure exactly what he was expecting the note to say, but I guess a small part of him was hoping it would say, "I love you Chad." Obviously it was wishful thinking, but Chad was a dreamer, to say the least.

All he really wanted was to have her back in his life because she was the person who held his heart; if he couldn't be with her in a relationship, then at least he would settle for a good friendship. As the school year continued on, their friendship began to pick up again. They spoke to each other more frequently, occasionally spoke on the phone, and acted as they did before this entire ordeal started. Eventually, they formed their own elite group of friends. It seemed that finally everything went back to being normal and that trouble had finally left the group.

As the school year came to an end, Chad and Alice went their separate ways during summer. Alice got a job scooping ice cream on the waterfront. They tried to stay in touch as much as they could, but between Alice working and Chad playing baseball, it wasn't easy.

Love can take you on a strange journey and Chad is having a hard time staying on course. At times loving someone means letting them go, and for Chad this was his daily reality. He would still dream of the day when he and Alice would be together, but he knew that this may never be the case.

CHAPTER VI

Growing Up

Most experts would agree that one of the most painful experiences one can have is unrequited love. One person can be completely and absolutely in love with another, yet the object of their affection either doesn't feel the same, or is completely unaware of their admirer.

If there was a dictionary definition to one-sided love, we'd probably see a picture of Chad next to it. With the start of eleventh grade, Chad and Alice were great friends once more. Chad was able to stand the fact that she was with Martin, yet still he kept on strengthening his bond with her and hoped that it could develop into something more again one day. Chad and Alice hung out frequently, strictly as friends, and there was no longer even an ounce of awkwardness. From the outside, it appeared as if nothing had ever happened between them.

As the year advanced, Alice eventually realized that Martin was still the same old jerk he had always been, so she decided to end things with him once and for all. She managed to get over Martin quickly, especially with Chad at her side. Her friends were very supportive as well and they all managed to turn her temporary frown upside down.

This time around, Chad was more astute with his intentions towards her. He had learned from his past experience that he might have come on too much like an obsessed stalker, and he decided to play it cool instead. Now that she was available, he had to plan his moves very carefully and needed to cut back on the over-the-top gestures that seemed needy and desperate. When someone is experiencing pain from a love wound, wisdom also begins to appear in the picture. Chad understood that love couldn't be forced; he knew that even though he was absolutely crazy about her, he would never be able to make her love him. It didn't mean that he would give up; on the contrary, his battle scars aided him in becoming a man more to the liking of Alice and he was determined to show her that he was the one.

He came to the conclusion that instead of going in for the kill, he would rather play the passive supporting role in her life. Instead of trying to win her over, he would only try to make her feel special and loved with hope that things might take a different path naturally. Alice did notice that he had matured, and that he was a sweet guy who really did care for her. She was very thankful to have Chad as a friend.

Their friends all knew how Chad felt about Alice, but they didn't make a big deal about it, because Chad no longer made a big deal about it. Chad managed to control his urges of jumping onto rooftops and proclaiming his love to her. He had learned from his past mistakes and understood that if he truly wanted her in his life, then he had to wait and prove that he was in it for the long haul.

Other than the glorious news of Alice's break up with Martin, there was nothing out of the ordinary that happened at school during the first half of the year. It seemed that everybody had their own personal agenda and that they were following it to the core. Obviously there were the many parties and binges, of which Chad enjoyed, and there were several girls that came in and out of his life during this time. Due to her volleyball schedule, Alice, on the other hand, couldn't attend that many parties. As the second part of the school year started, Alice's friend Tina had an upcoming birthday. There were no official plans made, but everybody knew that there was going to be a party. After school ended on her actual birthday, everybody went home and waited to see what was going to happen. Chad found himself at Jackson's house where they were waiting for the girls to call.

This was another lesson that both Jackson and Chad were about to learn about women: if you have to wait for their phone call, you might wait forever. As time continued at a turtle's pace and the day turned to night, the phone finally rang. Jackson went over and answered; the expression on his face told Chad that Tina was on the other end.

They spoke for a bit and then Jackson said, "We could have a few people over here if you don't find anywhere else."

One thing to note about Jackson is that he had a reputation for throwing some of the wildest parties in high school, and his meaning of a "few" could mean hundreds. The decision of the party destination did not bother Chad as he didn't have to go anywhere; he was already there. Thirty minutes later, there was a knock on the door. On the other side were painted up princesses ready to get their drink on. Less than twenty minutes later the door opened again, this time there were ten to fifteen people smiling and holding a wide array of booze. After the initial crew came in, the floodgates were opened and Tina's party at Jackson's house started resembling something like Spring Break at Daytona Beach. Jackson managed to not care after his third or fourth shot, and the party went into full swing.

Alice and Chad were hanging out most of the time, and Alice even wore his yellow Cal State hat. This made Chad feel all warm and fuzzy on the inside, or maybe that was the alcohol burning in his stomach … ? He almost felt like they were actually dating again in the way that they were laughing and just having the best of times. At one point, a sober friend drove all of them to 7-11 to get some munchies. Due to their inebriated state and indulgence in funny smelling cigarettes, they decided to play air guitar the entire trip with a complete disregard for onlookers. They had fun, to say the least.

As the night continued, Tina wanted to go meet up with some of her other friends. Chad tried to convince them to stay because if Tina left, inevitably Alice would leave as well, yet he failed miserably and off they went. Regardless, he was extremely happy with the way the night had gone. He had a great time with Alice, and she seemed to not really want to leave.

The relationship between the two really seemed to have gelled a lot better through the following months, until Alice dropped a bomb on Chad. One day she told him that she had started seeing someone new, Rory. This guy Rory was new to the school, and for some reason unknown to Chad, she decided to go out with him. Obviously, Chad's jealous side came out with all its usual fury, but luckily he also had enough wisdom to be quiet. "This is just a test," he muttered to himself.

Unlike Martin, Rory wasn't a total douchebag; in fact he was actually a nice guy. It's always harder to hate the nice boyfriend of the girl of your dreams, but Chad still had it in him. Still, he wasn't going to repeat his past mistakes, so he remained supportive of this new development, at least on the surface. Besides, last time he meddled with her last relationship they stopped talking for a year, so he was not going down that road again. This new approach really panned out for him; Chad and

Alice's friendship only became stronger as time continued. Even though Rory was in the picture, there was already something sacred about their relationship, something so unique that only they shared. For Chad this was more a test for himself than anything else.

At the end of the year another All Schools Dance at the Millennium building at Boban Park was set to take place. All of Chad and Alice's friends would be there. Despite being Alice's boyfriend, Rory didn't like these types of events and claimed it was because he was too cool for them, but the reality was that Rory never felt comfortable around Alice's friends. Rory had his own circle of friends who had a different set of interests. Chad didn't even think about Alice going without her boyfriend, he was more focused on meeting new people, especially girls. The night progressed without anything unusual occurring. At the end of the dance, Chad decided to start walking back home with a few of his buddies.

Across the way, in the grocery store parking lot, they spotted Alice and a couple of her girlfriends standing outside near the vending machine. They were trying to buy some more pop to mix with their vodka, which they had hidden in the bushes before they went into the dance. When they saw the boys, they invited them over in hopes of extending the party. Most of Chad's friends were already seeing double and graciously declined, but Chad was more than happy to go with the girls. There was no way that he was going to decline hanging out with a bunch of drunken girls. He was very curious as to where this night would end up.

They quickly attended a very forgettable party on the walk, stopped off quickly at Kari's house where they planned to sleep, and then made their way to Tim Horton's for an early morning snack. Out of the entire group, only one girl stayed at Kari's house and eventually fell asleep on the couch that was destined for Chad. When they came back, Kari offered her bed to Chad, yet what he didn't realize is that she actually meant that he could share the bed with her. Under normal circumstances he would be more than happy to jump into bed with a girl, but seeing that his true love was right there with him, he graciously declined.

Shortly after he declined Kari's offer, Alice offered him a spot on her bed which was more to his liking. They jokingly drew a line down the middle and got ready for bed. Even though Chad was bursting with excitement on the inside, he knew he had to keep himself in check because Alice wasn't the type of girl that would cheat on anyone. Due to their solid friendship, nothing happened that evening; they talked for a few minutes and then dozed off quickly into an alcohol-induced coma.

The next morning, she woke up before him and got ready for work. Before she could leave, he came down and said goodbye, got his stuff, and started walking back home. Even though nothing happened the night before, it was still a special moment, at least in Chad's mind anyways.

As the school year came to a close, he found himself to be in exactly the same position he was in at the start of the year. Alice had a boyfriend and he wished it were him. Just like the previous year, his love for Alice grew even more; however, this year he was more mature and went about the situation in a much more relaxed way.

As summer rolled by, Chad was chosen to represent his province at the national championships and had to leave for a month. Alice continued with her job at the ice cream shop, which meant that they were both very busy. They once more lived their separate summer lives and were destined to meet again the next year for their last year of high school. Twelfth grade is supposed to be the most exciting year in a high school student's life, and for Chad this was going to be his year.

One-sided love can be torture; however, this can change if both people grow together into something undeniably special. Chad and Alice were doing just that. Their friendship was strong and they had a mutual respect for each other that is rarely found amongst two people their age. Chad was finally becoming the master of his own heart, and with his newly acquired wisdom, things might change for him.

CHAPTER VII

A Sudden Turn of Events

Life, as most experts would agree, is based on cycles of constant change that each have a beginning, a middle, and an end. According to most high school students, their final year is idealized as an epic conclusion of all their collective experiences. Senior year ends in an ultimate celebration of freedom, accomplishments, and uncontrolled, adolescent hormones. Socially speaking, the Seniors are traditionally deemed to be the coolest, most experienced, and most idolized individuals in the whole school.

As Chad set foot onto school grounds for the first time as a Senior, he could feel a different air all around him. His excitement about his last year of "school" (aka perpetual boredom and useless information) was coupled with his belief that this would be a very special year in his personal life. Wherever he walked, he could hear one topic of debate surpass all of the others: the Prom. Even though it was the first day of school, it was all that the Seniors could talk about. People were already busy with finding dates and getting dresses.

Chad obviously wanted to take Alice, but seeing that she was with Rory, his chance was slim to none. In fact, it was mathematically more likely for a snowball to survive the flames of Hell than it was for Chad to take Alice to Prom. Chad decided to keep that topic on the back burner at least for the time being. Also, he knew that he had a surplus of females to choose from to go with him, so he wasn't worried.

At the beginning of the year, Chad and Alice only shared one class: English with Ms. Carrot, who also happened to be one of their friend's mothers. This gave Chad a buffer of tardy tolerance of which he happily took advantage. He made it a habit to oversleep on Mondays and Fridays due to his "extra-curricular" activities—drinking and partying. The remaining days he would gladly sit next to Alice and chat the class away. Ms. Carrot, even though annoyed at Chad's general lack of interest in her class, allowed his shenanigans to continue unchallenged.

The first half of that school year consisted of "preparing for college," which included excessive partying and drinking as far as Chad was concerned. Chad eventually did settle on a date he would bring to the Prom: Lacey. She was one year younger than him and obviously excited due to the fact that she would experience Prom twice; he was just happy that he had a hot girl to look good in the pictures with him. He still wanted to take Alice, but once again, the boyfriend factor stood in his way like a portly child barricading his Halloween candy.

As Christmas break was approaching, things started taking a sudden turn. Alice was ecstatic to spend her first Christmas with Rory. Chad was ecstatic to eat great food and not have to wake up early in the morning. The rest of their friends were also excited for their own reasons. They had all formed a tightly knit group over the years and were constantly in contact throughout their break.

On Christmas day, they all got together on MSN and started giving their seasonal greetings. Little did they know that the older they would get, the less important the "feeling of Christmas" would become, yet in their innocent ignorance they managed to "spread the Christmas cheer" by exchanging stories. When Chad inquired how Alice was doing, she responded with:

"Amazing; having a wonderful time with the boyfriend."

His heart, still emotionally attached to her, didn't appreciate these comments much, which only allowed him to respond with a flimsy:

"Great!"

The very next day, he received an expected phone call with an unexpected message. The phone rang a couple of times before he could answer it, and on the other side was Alice's best friend, Skyler.

"Hello, Chad?" Skyler asked.

"Hey, Skyler, Merry belated Christmas!" Chad responded.

"Merry Christmas! Hey, man, I have some news," she replied.

"What happened?" he asked.

"Rory just dumped Alice," she said excitedly, knowing that Chad was madly in love with Alice.

Obviously Chad was over the moon; he couldn't believe what he had just heard! Skyler assured him that this was the real deal and not a prank in any way. This was the best news that he could hear on Boxing Day; to Alice, on the contrary, it was unexpected and heart-wrenching.

Chad was now faced with a real dilemma: what was he to do? He heard only the night before that Alice and Rory were having a great time together, yet today they were broken up. Skyler continued to explain the story of how it happened and how extremely hurt and mad Alice was. Since Alice was in a very dark place, Skyler thought that Chad might be able to help cheer her up. A bittersweet victory was hovering over his heart, since he was both happy that she was single and sad that she was hurt. He decided to give her a couple of days to process everything. When he thought that enough time had passed, he decided to call her up. Instead of just finding out what was going on, he decided to invite her to a New Year's Eve party out in a suburb of town. She was glad that he called and whole-heartedly agreed to go. He also included Alice's good friend Ashlyn into the equation to make her feel better by being surrounded by her friends.

When New Year's approached, Chad went to pick up the girls with Jonathon, Bryan and Andy. This small group of high school Seniors had a lively agenda set for the evening, which commenced with a 60 pounder of Crown. Pretty soon they were all smashed out of their minds, seeing double and smelling like a fleet of sailors. It was in this drunken state that Alice decided to let go and started talking to Chad.

"I don't know why he broke it off… I mean, I thought we were having fun together," she said, slurring slightly.

They spent a couple of hours discussing the matter to death, while Chad was a complete gentleman and supported her through her heart break. After all, he was now an expert in the field of getting his heart broken so he thought that he could be a crutch in this dire time of Alice's need.

As the clock struck two in the morning, Chad and Alice decided to find their friends and try to figure out how they'll get back home. As Alice opened the front door, she was instantly hit with a blanket of ice cold air, which when mixed with enough alcohol can result in projectile vomiting. After scurrying around trying to find her shoes, she managed to make it outside and show the world what she had for dinner.

A man can tell if he is really in love when he sees that person in an unfavorable way and still finds that person attractive. With all the puke and tears, Chad still saw the angel that is his Alice; not even in her worst moment did Chad not love her.

Once she recovered from her spree, they both decided to continue with the search for their friends. Yet the more they looked, the more they realized that they might have left. They didn't show up at the rendezvous point, a local pub not too far away. Seeing that it was getting late, Chad decided to call his stepdad to come get them. After a short wait, they saw the headlights of his car approaching and got in. Chad's stepdad agreed to take Alice to her house first, before returning home with Chad. However they found that the trip would not be as smooth as they had hoped. Chad, who wasn't his normal loud self, was starting to feel his head spin. Soon enough, he abruptly demanded an emergency pull over. Chad ran behind the car and proceeded to show the world what he had for dinner that night.

Anyone who's throwing up when they're drunk knows you normally get a sudden sense of clarity and relief afterwards; likewise, Chad jumped back in the car and felt as good as new. He apologized to both Alice and his stepdad for his lack of control and sat back. Both renewed, they commenced chatting away the entire drive to Alice's house. Chad and his stepdad made it back home and upon arrival, Chad promptly dropped in his bed like a heavy stone.

The next morning he was awoken by a phone call from Jonathon inquiring as to what occurred the night before. According to him, they were looking for Alice and Chad the entire evening and couldn't find them. Eventually they came to the same conclusion that Chad and Alice did that night, thinking they had simply left. Chad explained his side of the story and they shared a couple of laughs. Jonathon also informed him that a little rumor had started circulating regarding the whereabouts of Chad and Alice on New Year's Eve. According to what Jonathon had heard, the pair went into the bushes to do more than just talk. Chad thought the rumor was humorous as it was completely false; however, he was afraid of how Alice would react. After talking to Jonathon, he decided to call Alice and share what he was just told. He hoped that she would find it as funny as he did.

Chad nervously told her everything, and without any sort or embarrassment or anger, they both had a great laugh. People eventually abandoned the idea of them actually having sex in the bushes, but that didn't stop their friends from ridiculing them for months about it. However, that night they grew closer. Their relationship continued to slowly evolve into something a bit more intimate. Chad was still very wary about this feeling as he had experienced it in the past before, to no avail. Thus he decided to continue with his plan to play it cool and see how things went.

The Christmas break ended as quickly as it began, and soon they all were back in school. However, it wasn't long after that things really started to get interesting for Chad. During the second week back to school, Chad and Alice were chatting over the computer late in the evening. After a long period of talking about nothing in particular, Alice dropped a bomb …

"So Chad, who are you taking to Prom?" she inquired.

"Lacey," he responded half-heartedly, since he really wanted to take Alice instead.

"Well, you should ditch Lacey and go with me instead," she responded quickly.

Chad froze in disbelief, stopped what he was doing completely, and started re-reading the message.

"Does she really want to go with me? Is this some sarcastic smart-ass humor?" he asked himself. He knew that this was something that could literally change the landscape of his entire Senior year, not to mention, fulfill his high school dreams. Chad knew immediately that this could not be discussed over the computer. He quickly rushed to his phone to give Alice a call.

"Alice, are you serious about the Prom?" he asked her over the phone, using his most confident tone … which still came out sounding nervous.

"Chad, I would love to go with you to the Prom," she said softly into his ear.

His heart stopped and so did his mind; this is what he had always wanted, this is the person who he has loved since the moment he laid his eyes on her, and all he wanted to say was "yes." The only problem was that he already had a date, and even though he was happy as hell, he now had to go and explain the situation to Lacey. Also, he didn't want to be Alice's second choice now that she and Rory were no longer together, so he had to ask:

"Alice, I don't want to be your sloppy seconds … you know, your back up plan," he told her.

"You're not; I would absolutely love to go with you as my first choice. That's what I've always wanted," she replied.

That response was enough to send him into a state of happiness that he had never before experienced. After sitting in silence for a few seconds, he quickly snapped back to enthusiastically accept her proposal. As he got off the phone, he could not stop thinking about that night. However, he did feel bad that he was going to cancel on his other date. Luckily, Lacey didn't take the news badly at all, especially since she was going to have her own Prom the following year. After being in love with Alice for more than four years, he felt like he had just beaten Goliath. There was nothing that could possibly bring him down from the high that he was feeling. He could not believe that after all this time, Alice has finally realized that Chad had the possibility of being more than just a friend. What he didn't know, however, was that he always had a special place in her heart and that in some ways, she had always loved him, even though she didn't realize it. He needed to show her that he was no longer a ladies' man. He could commit to one girl and give her everything that she deserved, especially if this girl was Alice.

Only a few weeks after this life-altering experience, Landon, one of Chad's good friends, asked if they could talk. Landon wanted to tell Chad that he also had a crush on Alice and decided to tell him about it out of respect. Chad never had a problem with Landon and he saw that this was not love; Landon simply had a regular high school crush on her. Landon never actually even spoke to Alice directly and always needed the assistance of a third party, which was generally Chad. Confident that nothing would come of it, since Chad knew that Alice didn't feel the same way about Landon, Chad stayed relaxed about the news. He figured it should be allowed to run its natural course; and this little crush would soon be gone and forgotten about.

February came rolling in and Landon decided to host a party in order to celebrate his birthday. As usual, the party got way out of control as these immature teenagers started drinking much more than they could handle. Not too surprisingly, Landon was the first to be out and was carried to his room before the party even officially started.

Chad, Tina, and Alice decided to go out for a walk to enjoy some of those funny-smelling cigarettes they enjoyed last time on Tina's birthday. Since it was incredibly cold outside, Alice took Landon's coat that was hanging in the closet by his front door. Not too long after they left, the party started dying out from too much drinking and too little self-control. People were vomiting all over the place, and upon their return from their walk, they understood why more people left. They were greeted at the door by Landon's mom yelling at the top of her voice. It seemed as though she wasn't too happy about all the puke and passed out teenagers in her basement, especially since her son was carried to his bed hours earlier. In her rage, she for some reason blamed Chad for a lot of the destruction and then out of nowhere agreed to drive Alice to her house. Chad, on the other hand, decided to walk home since he couldn't take any more of that crazy bee-otch.

Alice, on the other hand, had a very awkward car ride back as she had to spend fifteen minutes with an irritable and high-strung woman. The silence was eventually broken as she reached her house and quickly excused herself, giving a half-hearted "thank you" to Landon's harpy of a mother.

The peculiar nature of love can swiftly go from moments of utter despair to moments of ecstatic joy in mere seconds, like waves crashing in the ocean. Chad, who had thought that all hope was lost, suddenly got a second wind and now found himself closer to Alice than he had ever felt before. He was once again learning another major lesson on his journey: love is wild and very lively, no man can ever tame it. One can only go with it wherever it decides to take you.

CHAPTER VIII

Valentine's Day

Nobody can predict the future, but it is human nature to dream about the future and reminisce about the past, despite knowing that we have control over neither. The only time when we have any control over a situation, and a limited control at that, is in this present moment. Chad's present moments were still full of unfulfilled wishes about a future with Alice, but the year wasn't over yet and Prom was still to take place.

The day before Valentine's Day, Chad was talking on the computer to Krista, the younger sister of one of his close friends. They spoke every now and then, but they didn't really ever hang out as she was two years younger. They were inquiring as to what each of them was going to do for the commercial day of love. After finding out that neither of them had any plans, they both decided to go watch a movie together. This was better than spending the night alone anyways. To Chad this was only a harmless date, if you could even call it that, seeing that he had absolutely no interest in Krista whatsoever. Nonetheless, he went out and bought her a stuffed teddy bear just to make the day a bit more memorable for her. It was Valentine's Day and all.

The next day around 7 p.m., Chad went to pick up Krista. They went to a movie that was quite forgettable, which would not have been the case if it was with Alice instead. With Krista being his friend's kid sister, Chad simply enjoyed his time with her and made the best of the night. After the evening came to its uneventful conclusion, he dropped Krista off and thought nothing more of it.

A few days later, Landon walked over to Chad to tell him that he had invited Alice out to watch a movie. Alice confirmed Landon's outlandish claims, yet Chad did notice that there was something very different between the two stories. While Alice thought she was only going to watch a movie, Landon thought that they were going on a date. What Landon failed to tell her was that not only were they actually on a date, but in his mind he also believed they were now officially dating. The very next day he went over and declared the news to his friends. Alice didn't shoot him down because, to her, this wasn't going to go anywhere at all, so she played along for the time being to be nice. Just like that, Chad's love went from single to taken once more and he was left on the sidelines … again.

He didn't think too much of the relationship, as he knew that Landon and Alice could never work, and due to his past experiences he knew it was best to stay out of the way. As the week came to its conclusion, another All

Schools Dance was on the horizon and as usual Chad had his agenda in place. The night proceeded with its typical excessive drinking and inappropriate behavior between boys and girls. Chad was his natural self, except that this special evening had more in store for him than he expected.

Krista, his one-time Valentine's date, was following him around like a lost puppy. They wound up dancing a few times but nothing developed any further. He eventually decided to go outside and get some fresh air, and Krista was following right behind him. With her alcohol-hazed eyes, she confessed that she liked him a lot. He tried to explain to her that it wouldn't work between them and that he didn't feel the same way about her, but she ignored his words and went in for a kiss anyway.

In his intoxicated and horny state, he returned the kiss and allowed it to escalate into a long make out session. He did not think this through, as is the case of most men, and he did not realize the impact this had on Krista's heart. That evening when they both parted ways, he thought that nothing important had really happened; however, Krista, being a typical girl, made sure that it wasn't that simple.

Normally when he hooked up with someone he would get their number and never call them, but in this case he couldn't simply do that. He had to treat the situation with a bit more class than normal, seeing that this was his friend's sister. Krista kept on calling him the following week asking if they could go out, and since he didn't want to be a jerk, he finally decided to go along with it. He also thought that eventually she would realize that there would be nothing else to this relationship than what had already happened; however, he was on the verge of learning a new lesson in love. When two people spend time together they begin to form bonds, and these bonds become the foundations of their relationships. While he started spending a lot more time with Krista, his heart did something he did not expect: he actually started liking her. Not even anywhere close to love, but he kind of liked her. Krista was an attractive girl with a good personality, and suddenly the meaningless fling transformed into a relationship.

Chad also figured that maybe he should just go with it since Alice was in another relationship as well. For the very first time, both Chad and Alice were dating others simultaneously and both of their relationships were definitely strange; Chad was dating his friend's little sister and Alice was dating a friend she didn't really like. Looking closely, their closest friends could see that in fact there was a third hidden relationship, the one between Chad and Alice. Both of them spent more time with each other than with their "official partners."

Chad began to notice that Alice was changing her attitude towards him; she used a more personal tone when she spoke to him, and there was a special twinkle in her eye whenever she looked at him. Every time he entered the room, she greeted him with a soft touch and a warm smile. These signals were something that he had dreamed of since the first day he met her, and finally after being so patient, it seemed that something more was about to happen between them after all.

Alice and Chad both had a prior agreement to go to the Prom together and they both were going to honor it, despite the fact that they were both in relationships with other people now. Regardless, there is no way in the world that Chad was going to let anything, even a new girlfriend, stand in his way of taking Alice. Fortunately, neither Landon nor Krista ever questioned this arrangement since they both knew that Chad and Alice were old friends, and furthermore, their Prom arrangement pre-dated their existing relationships.

As February ended, the second semester was entering its second month. Chad and Alice found themselves in the same P.E. class, which was absolute heaven for him. Not only did he get to spend more time with his one true love, but he also could run around and show off to everyone how truly athletic he was. The first few months went great until there was a "situation" that occurred the week before Prom. (Most schools have Prom on the last day of school. This high school held theirs with a few months still left in the school year.) Chad and Alice found themselves playing cone ball, which in reality is nothing more than dodge ball with some cones scattered around as targets. Roughly half way into the game, Chad decided to turn up the heat against his opponents. He took aim at one of his competitors, who happened to be standing right in front of Alice. Chad hurled the ball with all his fury at his opponent, who immediately ducked out of the way, leaving Alice directly in the line of fire. The ball hit her right in the face and sent her flying to the floor. Chad's face turned a ghostly white as he rushed over to make sure that she was ok. Alice, highly embarrassed, rushed herself to the washroom while her face was throbbing from the impact of his rocket ball.

The only thing that went through Alice's mind was, "Please, dear God, don't let me have a black eye for Prom."

Alice would generally never worry about an injury unless it would make her look bad for a special event, and the following week was one of the most memorable events she would have in high school. She wanted to look her absolute best for Chad, and a black eye would definitely ruin her image. The ridicule from the rest of Chad's classmates was endless; they constantly kept on making fun of Chad for attempting to give his Prom date a black eye.

Chad felt wretched for hitting Alice; if it was some random chick he would have felt bad, but not like this. Alice was the real deal for him, and even though his friends were joking, their jokes really affected him more than they normally would. Luckily, Alice's skin was resilient and there was no black eye at all, although Alice would gladly remind Chad about this accident in the future just to "bust his chops," as they say.

Love is a game of joy and pain, sometimes emotional and sometimes even physical, but love is definitely the best experience anyone can ever have. Chad saw that his journey was starting to look a bit more promising, and with Prom on the horizon, he was jumping out of his skin.

CHAPTER IX

A Prom to Remember

At times, one's expectations of a special event or person end up completely different from what the event or person is truly like. We often hype up, or overanalyze situations like this, and once we are finally immersed in them, we find they are unable to live up to the standards we have created.

One of the most overanalyzed and overcomplicated events in a teenager's high school life is Prom, and with good reason. Prom generally symbolizes a turning point in a young man or woman's life, a transition from adolescence to adulthood. (At least in the eyes of these hormonal, slightly more mature than when they entered high school, students.) Chad's Prom was in May, a bit more than a month before they would officially graduate. Even though he wasn't entirely too caught up with the idea of Prom in the beginning, things had completely changed for him when Alice decided to make his dreams come true by asking him to be her date.

Using the rational side of his brain for once, he didn't expect that anything significant would happen between him and her that evening, since both of them were currently dating other people. He was just happy that he would be able to take pictures alongside the most beautiful girl he had ever met, and that he would have an excuse to dance with her whenever he wanted.

Before the actual event, they all got together at one of their friend's houses to take pre-Prom pictures. Alice, in her typical female nature, showed up an hour late due to an emergency hair disaster, which was probably blown way out of proportion as she had overstressed on this big day. What Chad didn't know was that she was taking extra measures to look her absolute best for him. While he was waiting, he took a couple of group pictures with his friends to pass the time. Once she arrived, his jaw almost hit the floor when her heavenly appearance completely took him by surprise. He always thought she was beautiful, but this new look definitely went beyond all his expectations. He was witnessing a dream of five years coming true right before his very eyes. At that moment time stood still. Everyone stood quietly as she exited the car door. It was obvious that it was not only Chad who was mesmerized by her beauty.

When everybody was ready to finally head to Prom, Chad and Alice got into his Toyota Paseo and headed for the hall. Upon arrival, they took pictures with friends and family until it was only the grads left. They all settled at their tables and waited for the evening to start; since this was a school event, there was no alcohol available, which meant they all acted like decent and respectful human beings for once.

When Chad and Alice stood together as a couple to have their picture taken, it seemed that almost everything he could have hoped for had come true. Yes, they were not officially going out, but here he was standing alone with the only woman that made his heart beat faster while making him want to be a better person, all at the same time. He now had many amazing photos with his dream girl that he would treasure for the rest of his life.

When the speeches started, the students began to discuss which after party they were heading to; too much time sober was damaging to their youth. They all danced for a couple of hours and then decided to really get the party going. At this point, Chad was very pleased with the way the night was going. Although he had such high expectations going in, he did not have any specifics that he thought would happen. He was simply overanalyzing the situation because he wanted it to be perfect. He created a unique memory with the girl he deeply loved, which they would always remember as their special moment.

The official after party was at Kris's house, and he had rented a hot tub for the occasion. Landon was there, and since he was technically Alice's boyfriend, Chad decided to mingle with other people and give them some room. After all, Chad did take Alice to the Prom whereas Landon went alone.

Chad's girlfriend at the time was sick in bed so she didn't join the festivities at all. However, that didn't stop other girls from trying to get his attention. One girl offered to have sweet lovin' with him in a limo. Normally he would have jumped at the opportunity, but he truly did want to change his adolescent ways, and the fact that he was dating Krista was further reason to reject the offer. He was now ready to take things more seriously and to create deeper lasting connections with people, as opposed to having casual sex in the back of limos.

The party ended sometime in the early morning and people went their separate ways. Chad ended up at a friend's house and went to sleep after everyone else. His mind was still reflecting on the night's events; he thought that something special must have happened between him and Alice. He felt different and was more confident than before that there was a real chance that she liked him the same way that he likes her. He knew that his patience was worth it; he understood that love can't be forced and if it was meant to be, then it would be.

Prom night turned into hangover post- Prom morning, and regardless of different people's experiences, there had been significant moments for everyone. Memories were made and hearts were changed, and for some, they could only look forward to disappointment at future events, as this one would be hard to beat. What we expect and what we get are often completely different; nonetheless, you can always be surprised to find that what you imagine regarding love will always be a gross understatement of what it truly is. For Chad, Prom alone was not extraordinary, but the precious moments spent with Alice were sweetly unforgettable.

CHAPTER X

Sparks at the Grad Camp Out

Who can predict the nature of one's heart? One moment you can love something deeply and in the very next moment you can despise its existence. Nobody knows what makes you fall in love with someone, or how it happens. All we know is that it happens, and hopefully we can learn to feel content with the way it happens.

Prom turned out to be a huge leap forward for Alice and Chad's phantom relationship. Even though Chad had to keep reminding himself that they weren't even dating, it sure as hell seemed that way. He slowly started losing interest in his current girlfriend Krista, and at just about the same time Alice started losing the little interest she had in Landon. Both Chad and Alice still found it very difficult to end things with the other people they were seeing however, which prolonged their dying relationships. One thing was for sure: Alice started having strong feelings for Chad, and not only did Chad notice, but his hopes grew higher about their future with every passing day. Chad eagerly anticipated the last two significant events in their high school lives where he and Alice would get to spend time together: the Grad Camp Out and Graduation day.

Grad Camp Out consisted of all the Seniors coming together on school property, partying their hearts out, and passing out in tents pitched all over the place. They would then wake up and go directly to class for their final day. Even though there were specific school regulations prohibiting this action, everybody always turned a blind eye to the annual event. It was a school tradition, something that every twelfth grade student should experience. Luckily, no adults who were overly conservative and completely out of touch with today's youth had banned it yet. Also, no unfortunate accidents had occurred to cause any concern about it; therefore, the Grad Camp Out tradition was still going strong.

That particular year, the camp out was going to be on a Thursday since the last day of school was on a Friday. Everybody was planning out what they were going to drink and what they would do to keep themselves busy throughout the entire evening. As soon as school finished for the day, people rushed over to their houses to prepare for the evening. Some people showed up as early as 5 p.m. to get everything ready while the rest trickled in later. Not everybody was planning on staying the entire evening, as their beds were way more comfortable than a sleeping bag; however, this was somewhat disappointing to others, as it is called Grad Camp Out. The night started out surprisingly peaceful until the alcohol blood ratio was breached. Once people were sufficiently drunk, they decided to go prank another local high school that was having their own Grad Camp Out on the other end of town.

These pranks ritualistically consisted of drive-by eggings. The first round came out a great success, but under their alcohol-filled reasoning they decided to do a second round. This time the other students were prepared and retaliated the attacks. As most practical jokes go, this one escalated and eventually the eggs were replaced with rocks; the other students didn't appreciate this very much and started hurling beer bottles at the car. As one beer bottle flew in the direction of Chad's head, which was popping out of the sun roof, he had to do a quick maneuver to not get hit in the face. His friend Adam wasn't so fortunate, for when Chad attempted to dive out of the way, he left his friend in the direct line of fire. Adam took a beer bottle to the face and left with a chipped tooth. This was the turning point for the evening, and the guys decided to head back to school before things got any more out of hand.

When they got back to the camp out, the girls were waiting for them. The boys filled the girls in on all the messy details and continued partying on. Chad and Alice weren't together much in the beginning, but as more people left, the space between them grew smaller. Eventually when the clock struck 1 a.m., there were only four campers left. Chad, Alice, Adam, and Alyssa all decided to go through with it and stay for the entire evening.

Chad and Alice decided to go for a stroll together around the school grounds. They didn't speak about anything specific, but there was a lot of flirting in the conversation. By this time, both of them had developed real feelings for each other and it was starting to become obvious to others. Chad understood now that something really had changed for Alice; she definitely had feelings for him. Due to their current relationship status, they couldn't do anything much about their feelings, even though they both really wanted to; therefore, they only walked around, talked and flirted.

It was extremely hard for Chad to be focused on the conversation because his mind was painting pictures of their future life together. His heart was beating a mile a minute, and he sensed that hers was beating exactly the same. In this moment, this conversation was a clear sign to him that he was right all along … this is the person he is supposed to be with. Seeing that in the past he had been wrong, he decided to cautiously see how this would evolve instead of his usual over analysis of the situation. After an hour or so of aimlessly wandering around, they decided to meet back up with Adam and Alyssa.

They decided to assemble one tent for all four of them to sleep in, and put it directly in front of the school in order to show everyone what they accomplished. Since there was only one tent, this meant that Alice and Chad would once again share the same sleeping space, except this time, Alice was excited as well.

Alice found a space right next to Chad and snuggled up against him. His heart and body were now completely out of control; he didn't want to fall asleep at all. He rejoiced in knowing for a fact that she had feelings for him; there would be no way that she would have been so close to him if she felt otherwise. While she lay there, he began stroking her face and hair and told her stories just to keep the conversation going. She reached out and touched his face, then looked deeply into his eyes. Automatically his arms wrapped around her like a blanket, and every passing minute was pure ecstasy for him.

Not long afterwards, Chad watched as she started drifting away. He couldn't contain the joy he had deep inside him. As she completely dozed off, he couldn't resist saying what he felt out loud, so when he was sure that she was out he spoke softly into her ears.

"Alice, you probably don't know this ... but I love you. I have loved you since the very first day that I saw you. There is no explanation why, nor is there a need for one. For the past five years, I have had feelings for you that are completely indescribable. One day, I would like to tell you this when you are awake. But for now, I'm afraid ... I'm afraid that you might not feel the same. You're my everything Alice ... I love you," he whispered.

Chad just had to get that out; it was bubbling in his heart for almost five years. He would never dare to speak about this without being absolutely sure that she felt the same way; he did notice she smiled a bit when he was saying it, almost as if her heart was listening while she slept. He knew that somehow she heard him, and from that moment he felt a huge weight lift from his shoulders.

As the morning came, they all woke up almost at the same time. They decided to go get cleaned up at their separate houses and to come back a bit late for their last day of school. That night was a dramatic turning point for Chad and Alice's relationship. They shared honest and open communication, and for the very first time ever, Chad truly believed that they now had something special together.

Chad also realized that he had to break it off with his current girlfriend; he simply couldn't continue to lie to himself anymore. He knew that the following year he would be in college and that a relationship with a highschooler just wouldn't work out anyway; furthermore, he wanted to show Alice that he was available. There was no other logical choice but to end things with Krista.

He was almost positive that Alice did have feelings for him now, and he was determined to follow up on that. He also wondered what had made her start to fall for him, since he didn't think he had changed much at all, but in the end, he didn't really care why. For the first time in his whole life, he felt certain that there was much more to come for him and Alice; in his mind, he had reached a new turning point in his life.

We will never know what motivates someone to love someone else, and we cannot control what our heart wishes to do. Chad was harshly placed in a situation where he would love and wait until that one day when Alice's heart was ready to love him back. Finally, he knew that possibility was slowly turning into a reality. His patience, heavy heart, and constant overanalyzing were finally going to be all worth it. We are all subject to the poisoned tip of Cupid's arrow at some point, yet only the brave will stay in the fight to win the war.

CHAPTER XI

Truly, Madly, Deeply

When one cycle ends, another always begins. Chad could sense that he was now in between two love stories: one needed to end and the other was about to finally blossom. He now had completely lost interest in Krista and knew that he had to break up with her soon. After some deliberation about when, mainly because he was scared to do so, he finally had the balls to break up with her on his graduation day. That morning he called her up and told her how he really felt; at first the news hit her like a freight train and she said nothing, but eventually her tear gates burst open. He felt like a complete tool, but he knew that he had done the right thing; it wasn't fair for Krista to be with him if his heart was somewhere else. However, he did choose a terrible day, as Krista was going to graduation to watch her brother and would also have to painfully sit through the ceremony while staring at Chad.

Over the short period of time that they were together, Krista had fallen deeply in love with him, at least in her mind. Krista finally knew how it felt to be Chad, loving someone and not getting the same love back. When they arrived at the graduation ceremony, Krista gave Chad a big hug and started crying. He tried to comfort her by promising that she'd find love again and that it was the best for both of them; however, the fact of the matter is that a broken heart is impossible to fix with words. He knew that she would have to ride the pain out and eventually grow from it. Love is not for the weak-hearted and if you dare to put yourself out there, you should be prepared to suffer the consequences.

The graduation ceremony itself was quite boring. It was simply a few students giving speeches followed by mindless applause and the periodic name-calling as some received their high school diplomas. Luckily, Chad's graduating class had just over 100 people, which didn't take too long to get through. When Alice's name was called, he fixed his eyes on her and was excited when she glanced over and smiled back at him.

Her smile now had a huge impact on him, much more than before. He would turn all warm and fuzzy when she looked at him, and it was almost as intense as the first day he met her. As she received her diploma, everyone around her disappeared from Chad's line of sight. He only saw her hallowed presence, illuminated with lights shining down from Heaven itself.

After everyone got their diplomas, most people went back home to prepare for the Dry Grad Party. The Dry Grad is basically an event thrown by the district's parents group with absolutely no alcohol, hence the name Dry Grad. It was a huge event because they invited grads from all the local high schools to come together for one massive party. Upon arrival, everybody would receive their entry bracelets and begin to party and dance throughout the evening. This event started around 6 p.m. in the evening and went until 8 a.m. the next morning. Many local companies would donate games and prizes to make the evening unique and exciting.

Chad arrived just after 6 p.m. with several of his best guy friends and they stood in line to get their bracelets and check in. Everybody was screened for alcohol and drugs prior to receiving a bracelet. The rules of the event stated that no one could enter without a bracelet, and if you chose to leave, then you were not welcome back. Upon entering, the guys quickly found the girls and started to make a plan for the night. Even though there were tons of people in the area, Alice and Chad managed to spend most of their time together. Despite the fact that she was still with Landon, and he was at Dry Grad too, it seemed apparent to anyone looking on that Chad and Alice were the actual couple.

Throughout the night, their interactions became more intimate as their flirting escalated into something new. It seemed that Alice was wholeheartedly looking at Chad the same way that he saw her; there was something quite new and different about her. She hardly saw her boyfriend that night and only went to him when she felt guilty for spending so much time with Chad. When Alice and Chad were not together, they enjoyed the night's activities with their other friends until they found a way to sneak back together. Neither of them had actually talked about how they felt to each other, which actually added to the excitement by not knowing.

They stood together in line to see the psychic, and the only reason Chad agreed was because it was long enough to give him alone time with Alice. He didn't really believe in what psychics claim to know since they generally gave out very ambiguous information that could be interpreted by anyone as personal. Messages like, "I can see that you are a kind person," or "I see someone in your future," never really struck Chad as mind-blowing. Once they both went and saw the psychic, Chad had his disbelief confirmed once more and they met up with a few others on their way to the dance floor.

As opposed to the traditional All Schools Dance, this party was lacking one fundamental element: booze. Even without the booze, people were still going wild and getting far too close to one another on the dance floor. Because this was probably the only time that he was completely sober at one of these events, Chad had a shocking revelation: he was actually a terrible dancer. It is funny how in one's inebriated state you can have a disillusioned sense of your actual abilities. This is a very

92

important life lesson for every one of all ages to be aware of; unfortunately many people, adults included, have yet to realize this.

As the night unfolded, Alice found herself next to Chad almost as if she had a magnetic pull towards him. Her feelings for him had evolved to something different; she finally could see him for the thoughtful, loving young man that he was. Unlike your typical high school crush, Alice and Chad already knew each other extremely well, so they knew exactly what they were getting into. They had already worked on, and strengthened, the most important aspect of a relationship: the friendship.

Even though they both had strong feelings for each other, they still couldn't fully express themselves yet due to the whole Landon situation. The pseudo-relationship of Alice and Landon was a joke, because they never hung out, talked or actually acted like a couple. Everybody knew that Chad loved Alice and some people knew that she was falling for Chad, but due to their social circle nobody really said anything about it. It was obvious to everyone who should have really been dating whom. Chad and Alice didn't do anything physical that night, but emotionally they were creating deep connections that would never be broken. They were actually building the foundation of a long lasting relationship, something much more sacred and pure than any physical action.

Near the end of the night, or morning by this time, there were prize giveaways of up to $5,000. Chad figured he had already used up all his luck on getting Alice's affection, which was fine by him as that was worth more than any monetary amount. They sat near the dance floor as the prizes were given away, paying little to no attention to what was going on around them. Her slight smile, body positioning, and gentle touches of his arm, showed how happy she was with the attention. For Chad, this once again turned into the best night of his life since he now felt even more confident that the woman he had been obsessing about for half a decade was truly falling for him. There was nothing more that he could ask for, and just as his high school career was coming to a close, he was starting to feel like this was turning into a storybook ending.

At the end of the event, he returned home and immediately crawled into bed. He lay there without being able to fall asleep; he was way too excited about what was happening in his life. He was no longer a high school student; he was on the verge of entering a new stage in his life and it appeared as though he may have someone to share the experience with. He knew that this upcoming summer could be a major turning point for his adult life.

During the summer, Alice actually asked Chad out after she finally, and painfully managed to officially break-up with Landon. Since they knew so much about one another already, their relationship transformed into something serious very quickly. The two of them had never been happier and felt truly blessed about how they both came to be together. They spent summer after summer laughing, loving, and playing. As the years went on, their love grew stronger. Chad was always amazed at how he could love someone more year after year, when he thought from day one that he couldn't possibly love anyone any more than he currently does. They established mutual values and goals, and they worked towards building a lifestyle and relationship that would make them truly happy for the rest of their lives.

On March 13, 2011, Chad and Alice professed their everlasting love to family and friends on a sun-filled white sand beach in the Dominican Republic. Chad had achieved his everlasting dream of marrying the only woman who makes him want to be a better man. For Alice, she married her best friend, a man who made her feel complete, a man who loved her unconditionally, and someone who spends every day letting her know just how special she truly is.

Even though some people attempt to capture the majesty of love on paper or in song, there is only one love story that truly impacts a person: their own. Chad was flung into the deep seas of love with a frail and ignorant heart, yet he managed to survive. If anyone claims that love is easy, they are mistaken; love is all about endurance, passion, and finding someone worthy of all the hardships that come with it. Love is about experiencing the victories and joys of your partner as your own, as well as giving support to the one who holds your heart in their hands. If you do fall in love, then really fall in love: truly, madly, and deeply. Revealing the deep secrets within your own heart and remaining vulnerable to your partner make love the most amazing and most painful experience one can ever have. If you don't believe me, just ask Chad...

Proposal Poem

Ever since I first saw you, that warm September day
I drove myself crazy, trying to figure out what to say

I was confused and excited, and a bunch of other things
For I had never in my life, expected to see an angel without wings

I will never forget when you walked in that room
My heart started racing at the smell of your vanilla perfume

Your beautiful blue eyes, your silky long blonde hair
I was 13 years old, and I almost fell off my chair

Your voice was so sweet, your smile so sincere
I began to sweat, I began to fear

What can be done to make my dreams come true
And eventually, having her say "I do"

I decided right there, these next 5 years would be amazing
By the time of graduation, it would be me everyone was praising

I worked really hard, and put my heart on the line
It took a long time, but she was finally mine

I swore from that day, I would never do you wrong
For I had the girl of my dreams, and our love was undeniably strong

As the years have passed, our love has continued to grow
It's perfect, peaceful, and precious just like a fresh layer of snow

We continue to achieve, things we thought we could only dream
We accomplish so much, because we make a great team

I look forward to our future, as I know it will be bright
As long as you are by my side, I know everything will be all right

Our love is one of a kind, and we have committed for life
The only thing that would make it better, is to have you as my wife.

Printed in Great Britain
by Amazon

44900563R00059